This book unfortunately belongs to:

_____

This book is dedicated to all of the characters and authors who try to scare others...including Joey Acker.

You should be ashamed of yourselves!

www.ackersbooks.com

Entire World Books: 2

Melanie was too scared to help write this book.

ISBN-13: 978-1-951046-00-2

The SCARIEST Book

in the Whole Entire World

Joey Acker

Hooray.

NOT!!!

Are you kidding me? Why do you want
to read the scariest book in the whole
entire world??

I am trapped in here, but you can turn back now!

Also, if you close this book, I won't have to go through the HORRORS again!

RATS AND CHEESE!!!

I thought you left!

Fine.

If you really want to know why this is the scariest
book in the whole entire world, I'll tell you...

Err...that's 3 reasons.

Just go with it.

Reason #2: I heard there was a ghost in this book.

Guess what?

I DO NOT LIKE

GHOSTS!

Oops.

I probably shouldn't be yelling in
a book full of scary things.

But do you know what really scares me?

REASON #3: SPIDERS!!!

NOPE!

Whew! Okay. What was next?

Ahhh yes.

Reason #4: I'm afraid of the dark.

Wait for it...

Hey! That wasn't so bad.

I guess I'm braver than I thought!

AHHHHHH!!!!

Hello?

Well, that's creepy and random.

Let me guess.

Reason #5: clowns?

Dude, I can totally see you.
My name is Bobo and I'm
here to help you.

Help?

Yep. I found the light for you and I'm supposed to give you reason #6...

THE
BEAST.

Oh yeah!

It's big, stinky, mean, has a scary horn on its head, AND I heard it eats spiders for breakfast and ghosts for lunch!

BEAST!?!

I don't remember any beast in this book!

What does it eat for
dinner?

. . .

ROCKS.

I'm a rock...

Wait! Where are you going??

Sorry, bro. I'm not sticking
around in this book.

Bobo out!

Reason #7: Bobo locked the door.

How am I going to get out of here??

And WHAT is that awful SMELL?!?

Grrrrrrrr

THE STINKY BEAST!!!

BOO!

THE GHOST?!?

Seriously?!?

Wow.

I don't think there is anything
scarier than a stinky beast!

Except for maybe a stinky...

Made in the USA
Monee, IL
16 September 2019